Thank you

Thank you for the food we eat;

Thank you for the friends we meet;

Thank you for our work and play:

Thank you, God, for a happy day.

My Book and My Name

_____

GOD'S WORLD
and JOHNNY

By Dorothy Westlake Andrews

Illustrated by Loraine Wenger

Rod and Staff Publishers, Inc.
Crockett, Kentucky 41413

CHRISTIAN LIGHT PUBLICATIONS INC
P.O. BOX 1212
Harrisonburg, Virginia 22801-1212
(540) 434-0768

Printed in U.S.A.

Code no. 83-7-96

GOD'S WORLD
and JOHNNY

In the Beginning

Johnny was a little boy who asked big questions. Oh, how many of them he could ask! From sunup to sundown, Mrs. Wade could hear Johnny's voice—"Mo-o-ther!" Sometimes it was Mr. Wade who heard—"Fa-a-ther!"

Outside the big white farmhouse where Johnny lived was a sign that read "C-L-I-C-K-I-N-G G-A-T-E." When someone would stop along the road and ask, "Why is your farm called CLICKING GATE?" Johnny would answer, "Because the gate clicks every time we open it."

Sure enough, "Clickety-click" went the gate as Johnny pushed it open.

One afternoon Johnny was hot and tired. His red wagon was very heavy. It seemed even heavier than when he pulled it down to the wheat field. He had taken a jug of lemonade and a basket of cookies for Father and the other men who were working there.

Johnny looked up the long lane, hoping he was near enough to see the sign, CLICKING GATE. But all he could see was the dusty road. It went on, and on, and on! He walked and walked. He pulled and pulled. But at last he came to the gate. He pushed his wagon aside, jumped up on the gate, and rode in as it sang, "Clickety-click."

Johnny walked around to the back of the house and found Mother sitting under the cotton-wood tree near the back porch. Close beside her was a big basket of mending. In the shadiest spot in the clover was a plate of fat, brown ginger cookies and Johnny's own special cup filled with cool milk.

"This is a stable for the horse that pulls a red wagon," said Mother, smiling at Johnny. "I even have some hay for my blue-eyed horse."

Johnny chuckled as he stretched out on the grass with a cooky in each hand.

"Can a horse eat hay lying down, Mother?" asked Johnny as he took a big bite out of the left-hand cooky.

"My horse can. He's a special kind," said Mother.

Johnny closed his eyes for a minute. When he opened them again, he could see the sunbeams as they danced through the cool green of the tree. Sometimes the wind blew its big leaves together with a soft, clapping sound. White clouds floated in the blue sky.

Johnny Wade had a happy feeling all over.

"Mo-o-ther, who made this tree?"

"Grandfather Wade planted it here, Johnny. He brought some baby trees from the flats by the river."

"Did Grandfather Wade make it grow?"

"He helped," answered Mother. "You see this was not a good place for little trees to grow, so he had to take extra good care of it. But mostly, it was the sun and rain and food the tree took from the rich ground. Even the snow helped a little."

"Then—did the sun and rain and snow make the tree?" Johnny still was not satisfied.

Mother smiled. She rocked for a minute, threading her needle with brown floss that matched Father's work socks. Then she said, "I know a book that will answer your question, Johnny."

Mother reached down in her big mending basket. Out of it she took a book. Johnny got up to see what it was. The book was black, and felt smooth when he touched it.

"I know. It's your Bible. Father told me how to read B-I-B-L-E." Johnny's finger marked each gold letter on the front. "But does it tell about our tree?"

"Yes, Johnny." Mother turned to the first words in the book. "It tells how everything began. It says, 'In the beginning God created the heaven and the earth.' "

"But does that mean God made the tree?"

"Yes. He thought about and planned the way it should come to be. He gave us the seeds, and the sun and rain, and men like Grandfather Wade to plant the right kind of trees in the right places. And just as God planned it, everything in the world came to be."

Johnny thought about this for a moment. Then, turning slowly, he looked all around.

Down in the barnyard stood Mara and her little colt, prancing a bit now on legs that were strong instead of wobbly. In the field beyond, two brown and white cows were contentedly grazing. In the pigpen, squealing brown bodies scrambled in the mud of the trough to get near their big lazy mother.

Johnny looked at Mother's vegetable garden with its border of gay flowers. He saw the hen house where every day he helped gather the eggs. Around it strutted the big red rooster, crowing proudly.

All these were part of God's plan.

"There are so many things," said Johnny.

Mother smiled. "That's why Father and I came back to CLICKING GATE to live. Father wanted you to know how everything begins. He says farmers are partners with God because they help things grow."

"Like cows and pigs and trees, Mother?" asked Johnny.

"Yes, and little boys." Mother smiled at Johnny as she closed the book. "We help them grow, too. But in the very beginning of everything, Johnny, there was God, His thought and His plan for it all."

Just then Johnny and his mother heard Father as he shut the gate—"clickety-click"—and walked up the path.

"Father," shouted Johnny, as he jumped into his father's outstretched arms. "I'm so glad God thought about us!"

Johnny's Best Day

Johnny thumped his head against the window-pane. "I wish it wouldn't rain!" he said.

"But we need the rain, Johnny," said Mother cheerfully. "It has been much too dry for my garden."

"But there's nothing to do!" wailed Johnny. "What can I do, Mother?"

"Let's see—I know. We'll make a book of all the people who help make this rainy day fun for us. They'll be very special people."

As Mother thought of the things they needed, Johnny went running to find them. There were magazines from the pile in the basement, scissors from the desk drawer, paste from Johnny's own workbox, and a big sheet of brown wrapping paper from Mother's paper and string shelf.

"Now what?" questioned Johnny eagerly.

"Now it's time for the mail," answered Mother. "Put on your raincoat and boots, Johnny, and go down to the box and see what Mr. Evans brought us."

So Johnny went down the lane to the mailbox, splashing in the puddles. He climbed up on the fence post by the mailbox, reached in for the mail and hurried back to the house.

"Two letters for Father, a paper for me, and why, Johnny, this box is for *you!* It's from Grandmother Martin."

Johnny could hardly wait until the box was open. In it was a shiny red and silver top. Over and over, Johnny wound it up and watched it whirl around the floor. At last his fingers were tired. He put it back into the box.

"Now, young man," said Mother, "we can begin our book. Who did something special for you today?"

"Grandmother Martin!" beamed Johnny.

"Then find a nice grandmother picture for the very first page," said Mother. "And how about the mailman? Didn't he bring your gift?"

"Oh, yes," said Johnny, turning pages as fast as he could, "the mailman's always bringing us things!"

The day went by so fast Johnny hardly knew it was raining.

He had just begun his book when there was a knock at the back door. There stood the man who hauled their milk to the bottling plant. Father had forgotten to unlock the door to the cooler so Johnny ran for the key. He liked to watch the man load the big shiny cans of milk.

"He's special, Mother," Johnny said as he came back to the table. "He brings us butter and takes milk to the other boys and girls."

Just before supper Mother's friend, Mrs. Carroll, brought in a big pan of hot rolls, smelling of brown sugar and cinnamon and butter. Johnny could hardly wait for supper. "But I'll have to find a cooking lady, Mother," he said. "Mrs. Carroll is the best of all."

"See my book, Father," said Johnny happily as his father settled down in his big chair after supper. Climbing up on Father's lap, Johnny turned the pages slowly. "It's the people who made today go fast," he said. "There are ever so many."

Father looked at all the pictures and the words Mother had printed under them telling how each one helped.

"It's a fine thing to have good neighbors, Johnny. They help us in some way every day. There's a special verse about them in the Bible. Perhaps Mother can find it for us."

So Mother looked in her Bible. Then she brought it to Father and he read the verse to Johnny. "Let's write it in the book, Son, and then off to bed."

Father wrote in big letters: "THEY HELPED EVERY ONE HIS NEIGHBOUR."

"I think I like rainy days best," said Johnny sleepily as Father carried him upstairs on his shoulders. "I don't care if it rains tomorrow and tomorrow and tomorrow!"

Johnny Learns About Breakfasts

Johnny took a big drink of orange juice. The sun, coming through the kitchen window, made it sparkle in the glass. It was all goldy yellow and cold and sweet.

"Mo-o-ther," said Johnny, "where do oranges come from? Father doesn't plant any."

"The ones that made your juice this morning came from Texas. Aunt Betty sent them in a big box on a freight train. They grow near her house."

Johnny thought about that.

"Does everything grow?" he asked.

"No," said Mother. "Some things are made by people."

"Like my overalls?" Johnny looked down at them. "You made them out of Father's."

"Yes, like overalls and furniture—and even some food. We don't always eat food the way it

grows,'' said Mother, who was beating eggs in a blue bowl. ''Someone had to make flour from our wheat before I could make you this chocolate cake.''

Just then Father came to the back door.

"Is there a boy here who would like a ride in the new truck?" he asked. "I have to take it down to the garage."

"Me!" cheered Johnny scrambling down in a hurry.

Father swung him up on the high front seat, and off they went to town.

At the garage Mr. Taylor opened the hood of the truck and began to pour in thick oil from a big can.

"Is the truck having breakfast, Father?" asked Johnny, thinking of his milk and orange juice.

"Yes," said Father as he started the motor and the big truck rolled down the road. "This truck needs oil and gas to make it run, just as you need milk to make you grow."

"Does the oil come from that big red can?" asked Johnny.

"It's a long story, Johnny. Deep in the earth God made and kept a black liquid we call petroleum. People make oil and gasoline from it."

"Pe-tro-le-um." Johnny said it slowly. Because he liked the sound of it, he said it over and over.

"Does it do other things, Father?"

"Besides being a breakfast for the truck? Yes, on our farm it makes our lights, runs Mother's stove for cooking and all the big machines in the barn. Sometimes we even take a little of it to oil the gate when it squeaks, instead of singing, 'Clickety-click.' "

"Did God know we needed it?"

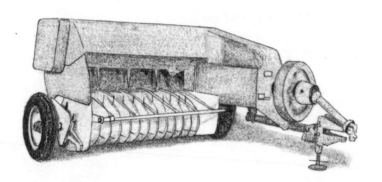

"I'm sure He did," answered Mr. Wade, "just as He knew you would need milk and orange juice. That's why we have cows in the meadow, and orange trees growing in the sun, and petroleum in the ground."

"Why don't we have oranges here, Father? Didn't God want us to have them?"

"Of course He did. But oranges grow better where the weather is warm, and wheat grows better where it is cold. Sometimes we have to share the things we raise the best. So we send wheat to Aunt Betty and she sends oranges to us. When we don't do our part, Johnny, somebody doesn't have a good breakfast like the one you had this morning."

"I wouldn't like that," said Johnny. "I love my breakfast, especially when Mother makes wheat cakes. One day I ate seven, big, puffy ones."

His father laughed. "I'll tell you a secret, Johnny. Once when I was hungry I ate thirteen."

"Father!" gasped Johnny. "Where did you put them?"

Father didn't answer—maybe because he was too busy driving the truck up to the barn, or maybe because he wondered the same thing himself.

  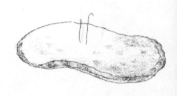

"Come on, Son. Let's see that someone gets a share of our food for breakfast tomorrow. I'll get the milk ready to be taken to the bottling plant, and you see how many eggs you can find."

"If I find thirteen, could you eat them all?" laughed Johnny as he ran to find the first egg.

Johnny Says Hello

It was snowing hard. After it stopped there would be fun for Johnny. There would be his sled and his new wooden skis to try, and perhaps Father would make him a snowman!

But right now it was warm and cozy before the fireplace. Mother had pulled the table and two chairs over near it, and she and Johnny were making "Hello" cards.

The first time they had made them Johnny had to ask Mother what "Hello" cards were for. And she had said, " 'Hello' cards are to tell our friends we remember them and love them."

As Johnny carefully cut along the black lines Mother had drawn he said, "Sister Mary told us a verse about friends last Sunday. It was 'A friend loveth at all times.' I know I love Lonnie all the time. He's my very best cousin. And Billy's my very best friend."

"Lonnie's away off in Texas and Billy has the measles," said Mother. "I think they would like a card each."

So Johnny took his crayons and the two white cards he had just finished cutting and drew some pictures on them. On Lonnie's he made a picture of snow, because Lonnie lived in Texas where there wasn't any. On Billy's card he made a picture of Tabby Gray's new kittens.

Then Mother helped him to print:

HELLO
FROM
JOHNNY

"Where else shall we send cards today?" asked Mother.

"To Grandmother and Aunt Betty," replied Johnny.

Johnny took a crayon and began to draw. He looked so worried that Mother said, "What is troubling you, Johnny?"

"I've made a picture of clicking gate for Grandmother, but I can't draw it clicking."

Mother laughed and laughed. "I'm sure Grandmother will remember how it sounds."

On Grandmother's card he asked Mother to print, "The top still spins, Grandmother, but the silver is gone", and on the other card, "We like our oranges, Aunt Betty."

Johnny put X X X X X's on the cards below the printing and then sat back in his chair.

"There are ever so many people to love, aren't there, Mother?" said Johnny.

"Yes, and ever so many to love us," replied Mother. "That's part of God's plan, too, Johnny. People can't get along without loving and being loved."

Johnny got up from his chair and went over to his mother. He put his arms around her neck and said softly, "I can't write it by myself, but I can say it."

And Johnny whispered in Mother's ear, "Hello, Mother. I love you!"

How Wonderful Is Johnny

"Mo-o-ther," asked Johnny, "what is the best thing God ever made?"

"I hardly know, Johnny." Mother stopped to think. "Why do you ask that?"

"Wel-l-l, the wind was making my pinwheel go. And I think my pinwheel is the best thing I ever made—so I was just thinking . . ."

"That's hard to decide, Johnny. While I think about it, suppose you run out to the barn and tell Father that supper will soon be ready."

Johnny hurried off to the barn, where he found Father mending a harness.

"Father, supper is almost ready and what was the best thing God ever made?" gasped Johnny all in one breath.

"Right now I'd settle for *you,* Son. But I didn't think so last week when you let the pigs out of the pen," he said.

"Did God make *me,* Father?"

"He surely did, Johnny. God planned the way of it, the way everyone is born. Mother and I were part of His plan for you. People are very wonderful, Son."

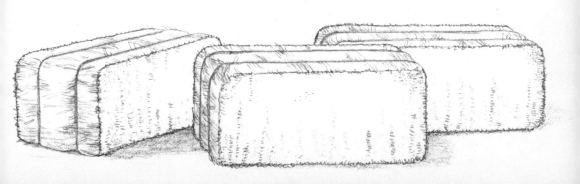

"Better than horses, Father? Better than automobiles?"

"Much better, Johnny. Let's play a little game and find out how wonderful you really are."

Father looked all around. At last he picked up something from his worktable.

"Close your eyes, Johnny, and keep them closed. Now take this in your hand and tell me what it is."

Johnny's hand opened and closed.

"It's a nail, Father," he exclaimed as his eyes flew open.

"That's right," said Father smiling. "How did you know it was a nail?"

"I could *feel* it," said Johnny.

"And you remembered what a nail feels like. Automobiles can't feel or remember. Close your eyes again. Now can you tell what I am holding near you?"

"Hay!" declared Johnny. "I can *smell* it."

"What color is my sweater?" asked Father.

"Blue," said Johnny. His eyes popped open. "I can see it."

"Turn around," was Father's next order. "Now what am I doing, Johnny?"

Johnny listened.

"Sawing—sawing a board," he cried. "I can *hear* you."

"This is the best of all," laughed Father. "Close your eyes and open your mouth. Now what have you in your mouth?"

"A peppermint!" Johnny could hardly talk because he was laughing and chewing at the same time. "O Father, I like this new game!"

"It's called, 'How Wonderful Is Johnny! "
said Father. "God made you to feel, and smell,
and see, and hear, and taste. Automobiles can-
not do any of these things, Son. Dogs and horses
can. But you have an *extra* gift from God, Johnny,
which He gives only to people."

"What is it, Father?"

"You can choose, Son. You can say yes or no.
You can do bad things or good things. You can
decide what is best."

"Like letting the pigs run away?" Johnny was
really sorry about that. It had taken Father all
afternoon to catch them.

"Yes, Johnny. And good things like sending your top to Billy when he had the measles, and you knew it couldn't come back to you."

"Is it very special to be people, Father?"

"It is the most important thing in the world to be *good people*," said Father seriously, "the kind God wants us to be."

Father put away the harness tools. "Come on, Son—the best thing for us right now is to be on time for supper."

Johnny Keeps the Measles

Johnny was as sick as he could be, for Johnny had the measles. Now, after all his friends had had them, after Billy was well again and ready to play, *Johnny had the measles!*

Johnny's eyes were red and swollen, so the shades had to be pulled down. There was nothing to see, and if there were, he couldn't see it.

He itched all over, but his hands were tied up so he couldn't scratch himself *at all.*

He was hungry all the time, but nearly every time he said, "I want something to eat!" Mother answered, "I'm sorry, Johnny not just now."

When Johnny said, "I want to get up,"
Mother replied. "Not until your fever is down,"
and popped a thermometer into his mouth!

And when Johnny wailed, "I want something to play with!" Mother said quietly, "You must be very still, Johnny, until you are better."

And because Johnny didn't sleep very well, this went on all day and almost all night. Mother began to look tired and pale. But never once did she shout at Johnny or talk crossly, and never once did she cry as Johnny did almost every day.

"Be careful, Mrs. Wade," Johnny heard the doctor say one afternoon. "You'll be in bed yourself. Measles are bad at your age. And since you've never had them he can give them to you easily."

Johnny thought about this for a long time. He never had anything he so much wanted to give away as the measles!

If he gave the measles away, he could see.

If he gave the measles away, the itching would stop.

If he gave the measles away, he could get up and play with Billy, and have something really good to eat.

"Anybody can have the old measles," thought Johnny.

But the only person to give them to was Mother. No one else came to Johnny's room except the doctor. Somehow Johnny was sure you couldn't give "being sick" to doctors!

So Johnny thought about Mother and the measles. His happy, pretty mother. *She* would have the sore eyes and the itching hands. *She* would be hungry and have to stay in bed.

Who would take care of Father?—and the house?—and Johnny? Everything and everybody needed Mother.

The next morning when Dr. Brown came into the room, Johnny frowned at him.

"I could, but I won't!" he said firmly.

"What won't you do?" asked Dr. Brown.

"Give Mother the measles," said Johnny. "I could easily—you said so. But I don't want Mother to have the measles. I'd rather keep them my own self."

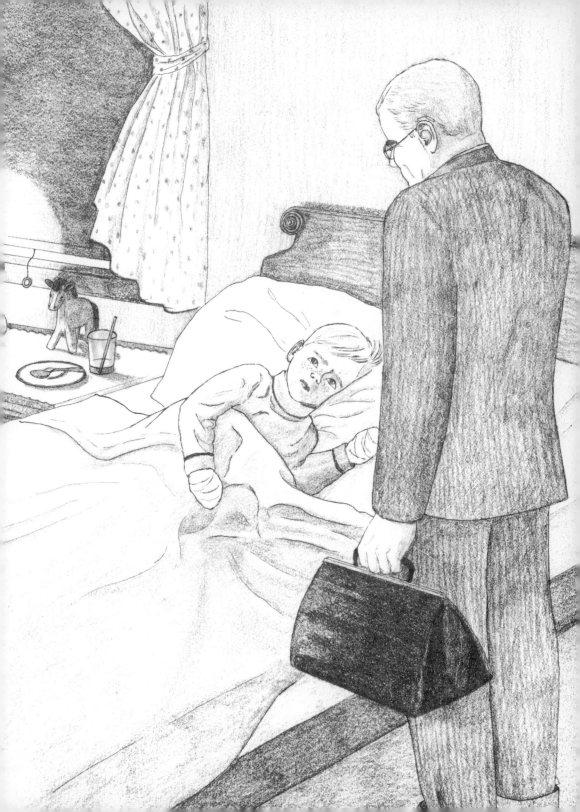

Johnny didn't know why Dr. Brown patted his shoulder.

He didn't know why Mother cried a little, and said, "O Honey, I love you so much!"

But he *did* know why Father said something special when he came to the door to say "good night." For Father said, "I'm very pleased with you, Son. I know I can count on you to take care of Mother now."

And Johnny Wade felt almost as good as if he'd never had the measles at all.

Our Family

It was Sunday afternoon. Johnny and Father walked along the river looking for a willow branch to make whistles. It was harder to make them after the sap stopped running, but Father always managed somehow.

The leaves of the trees were like the bright colors in Johnny's paint box. But Johnny didn't even notice them, for he was very unhappy. His favorite family of robins had flown away, leaving an empty nest.

"Father," said Johnny, as his eyes filled with tears, "why did our birds go away?"

Father's knife flashed as he cut a short piece of willow and began to loosen the bark.

"Do you remember how the mother and father birds built their nest here?" he asked.

"Oh, yes," said Johnny, almost forgetting to be sorry. "They took the string you tied the vines with, and Mary Jane's blue ribbon when she left it on the porch."

"But now they know that winter is on the way," continued Mr. Wade, "and that it's time to take their family to the South, where it will be warm."

"Are birds really a family—like us?"

"Yes, they are, Johnny. The mother and father birds built their nest here in this tree. They made it as carefully as they knew how. That's just the way Grandmother and Grandfather Wade made the farm many years ago. They wanted their children to have a safe comfortable home."

"Then," Johnny went on excitedly, "the birds had some children, too. I saw the eggs in the nest, but I had to wait such a long time to see the little birds. They had four children, Father, but there's only one of me."

"Yes," laughed Father, "but someday you'll have that brother and sister you've been asking for. Then Mother and I will have a nest full, too!"

"Why did the father bird have to get food for them all the time?" asked Johnny.

"God's plan was for families to have children and to take care of them while they are young. That's why Mr. Robin had to work hard to find berries and seeds to carry to his babies," answered Father.

"Did you help feed me?"

Father laughed. "You were so little I was always afraid I'd drop you. Your mother took very good care of you, and I helped when I could. I taught you to walk, Johnny. How happy we were the day you took your first steps!"

"The father bird helped his children to fly," said Johnny. "I watched them."

"Yes," said Father. "First he let them climb to the edge of the nest. Then they hopped out on the limb, and he showed them how to spread their wings and fly to the ground or to another tree."

"The mother bird kept hopping up and down, making funny noises," said Johnny.

Father laughed. "She was afraid they might fall, just as Mother was when you took your first steps. Mothers and fathers are always a little worried about their children until they know that they can take care of themselves."

"I liked hearing the birds sing," said Johnny. "First they said, 'Chee, chee,' and then they all sang a big song. It was, 'Chir-up, chir-up.' I guess they were happy."

"Families should be happy, Johnny. That's the way God wants them to be." Father made a last cut in the whistle. "Here, son, see if *you* can make a song."

Johnny tooted softly on the whistle, but somehow it made him feel a little lonesome.

"Will the birds come back?" asked Johnny.

"Only the father and mother birds will come back here, Johnny," answered Father. "You see, before they go, the babies grow big enough to fly anywhere and get their own food. Then they are what we call independent. Next year each one will have a family of his own."

"Will I be in-de-pen-dent when I'm big?" asked Johnny.

"Yes, Johnny. Every day you are learning to do more things by yourself, to think and choose wisely. Some day you'll have a family of your own to take care of, perhaps right here at CLICKING GATE."

"I'll make them all whistles," said Johnny happily, as they started home to Mother.

And that's how Johnny by asking,

WHAT?

WHY?

WHEN?

WHO?

found that the answer to his

biggest questions was always

GOD.